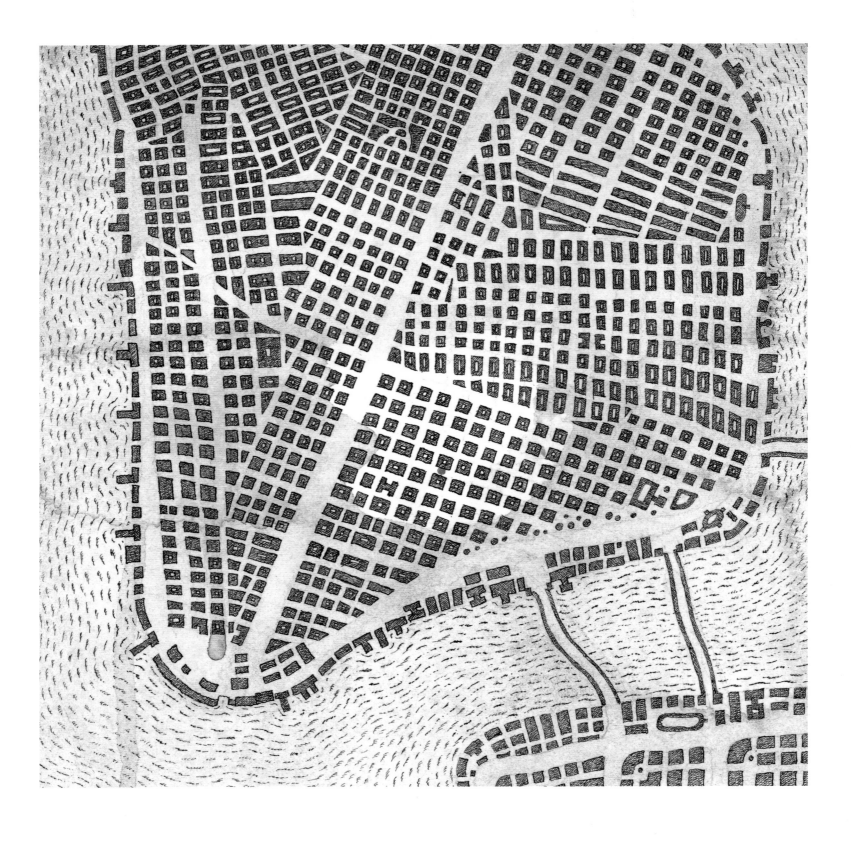

MADLENKA

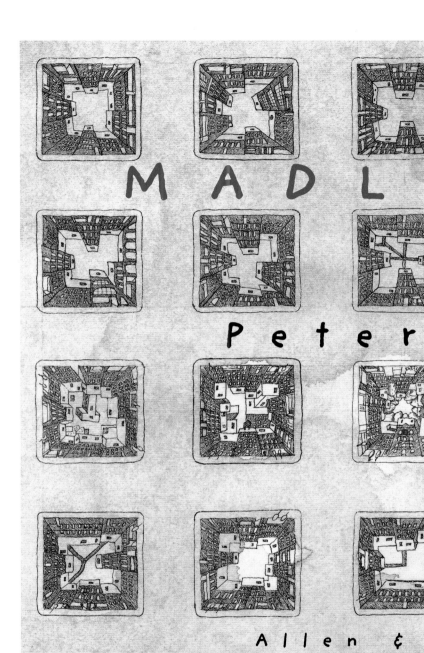

Peter Sís

Allen & Unwin

In the universe, on a planet, on a continent, in a country, in a city, on a block, in a house, in a window, in the rain, a little girl named

Madlenka

finds out her tooth wiggles.

She has to tell everyone.

Hey, everyone . . . my tooth is loose!

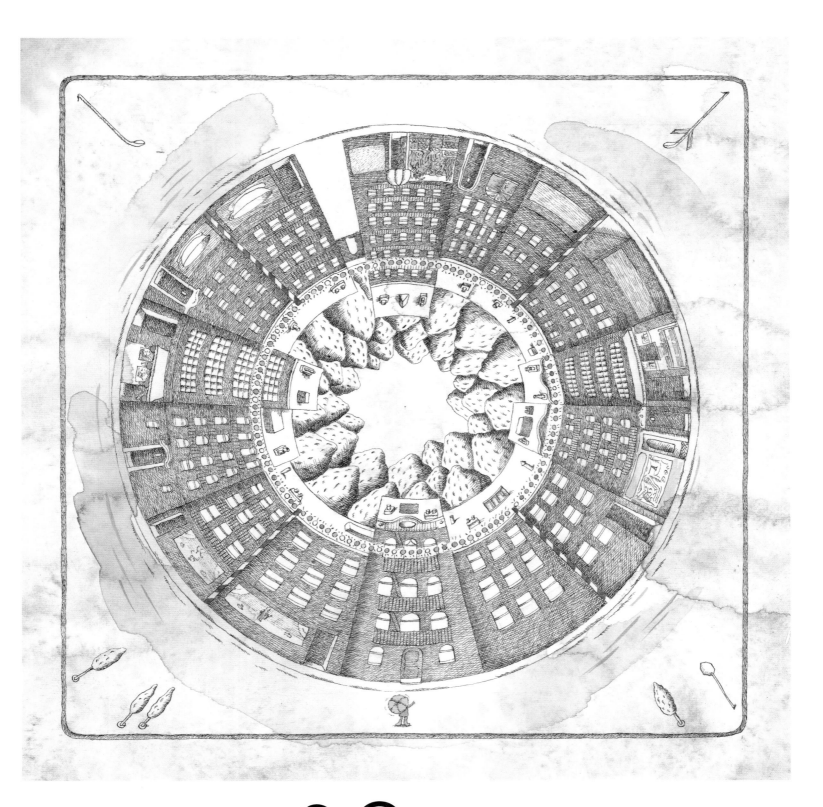

LO O O S E

Jumping with joy, she skips down the street
and sees her friend Mr. Gaston, the French baker.

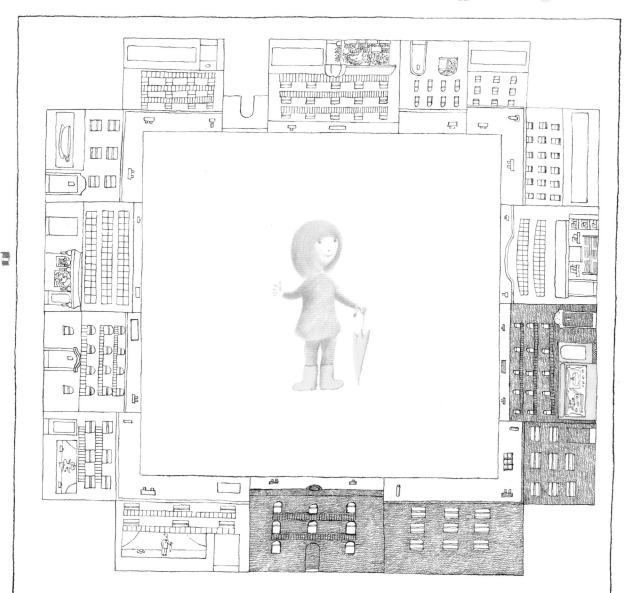

CROISSANTS

MADELEINES

CHOCOLATE CAKES

FRENCH BREAD

CAKES WITH FRUIT

FINANCIERS

WHEN I HAVE A BIRTHDAY HE PUTS A PINK BALLERINA ON MY CAKE ....→

HE TELLS ME ABOUT PARIS

AND ABOUT FRANCE

MR. GASTON BAKES

I AM A BIG GIRL NOW

HELLO, MR. GASTON — MY TOOTH IS LOOSE!

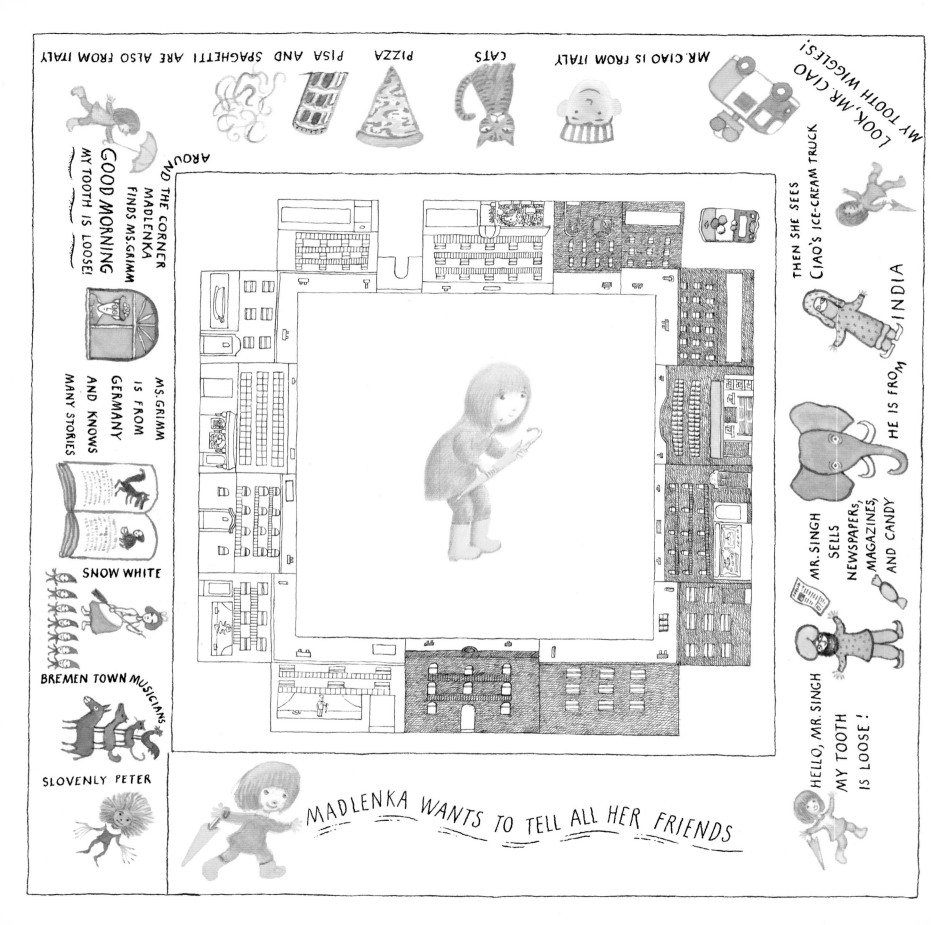

PISA AND SPAGHETTI ARE ALSO FROM ITALY

PISA AND

PIZZA

CATS

MR.CIAO IS FROM ITALY

LOOK, MR. CIAO
MY TOOTH WIGGLES!

GOOD MORNING
MY TOOTH IS LOOSE!

AROUND THE CORNER
MADLENKA
FINDS MS.GRIMM

MS.GRIMM
IS FROM
GERMANY
AND KNOWS
MANY STORIES

SNOW WHITE

BREMEN TOWN MUSICIANS

SLOVENLY PETER

THEN SHE SEES
CIAO'S ICE-CREAM TRUCK

HE IS FROM INDIA

MR. SINGH
SELLS
NEWSPAPERS,
MAGAZINES,
AND CANDY

HELLO, MR. SINGH
MY TOOTH
IS LOOSE!

MADLENKA WANTS TO TELL ALL HER FRIENDS

Sathsariakal, Madela. Good news!

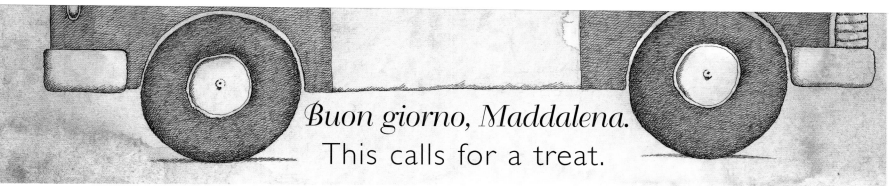

Buon giorno, Maddalena.
This calls for a treat.

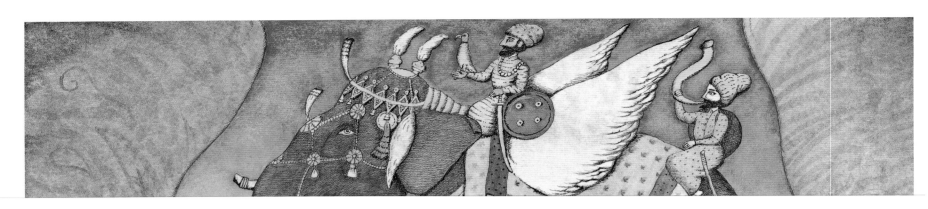

Madlenka thinks this must be the best day of her life.

Oh, there's Mr. Eduardo, the greengrocer.

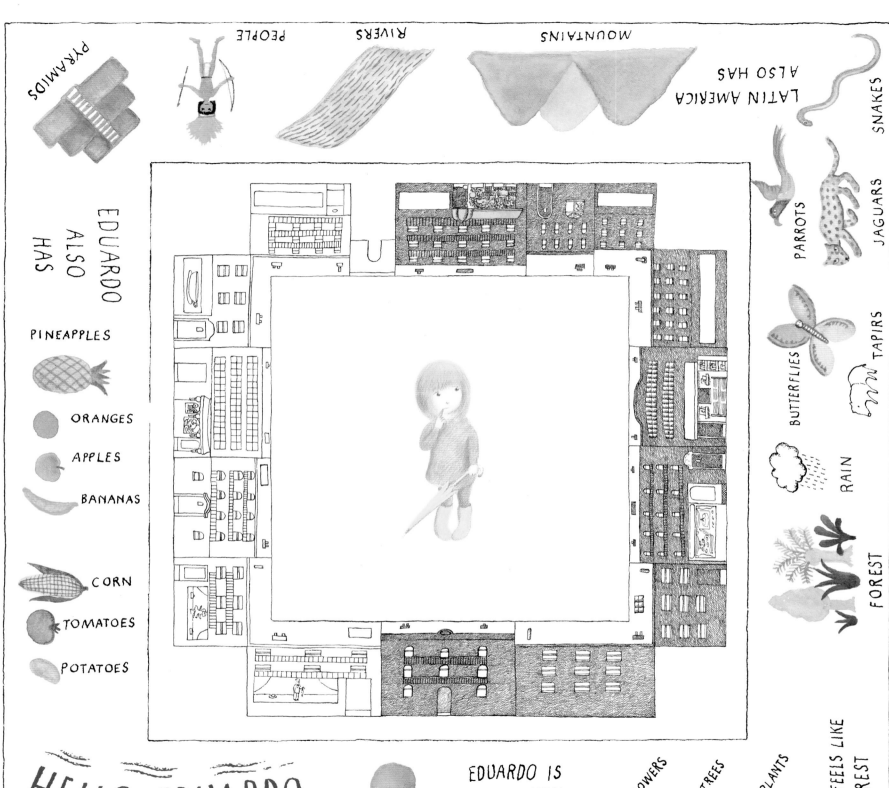

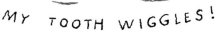
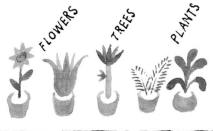

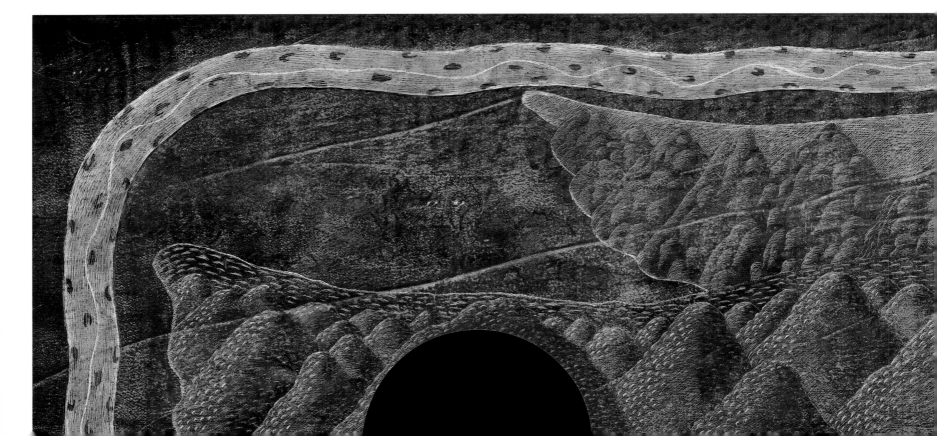

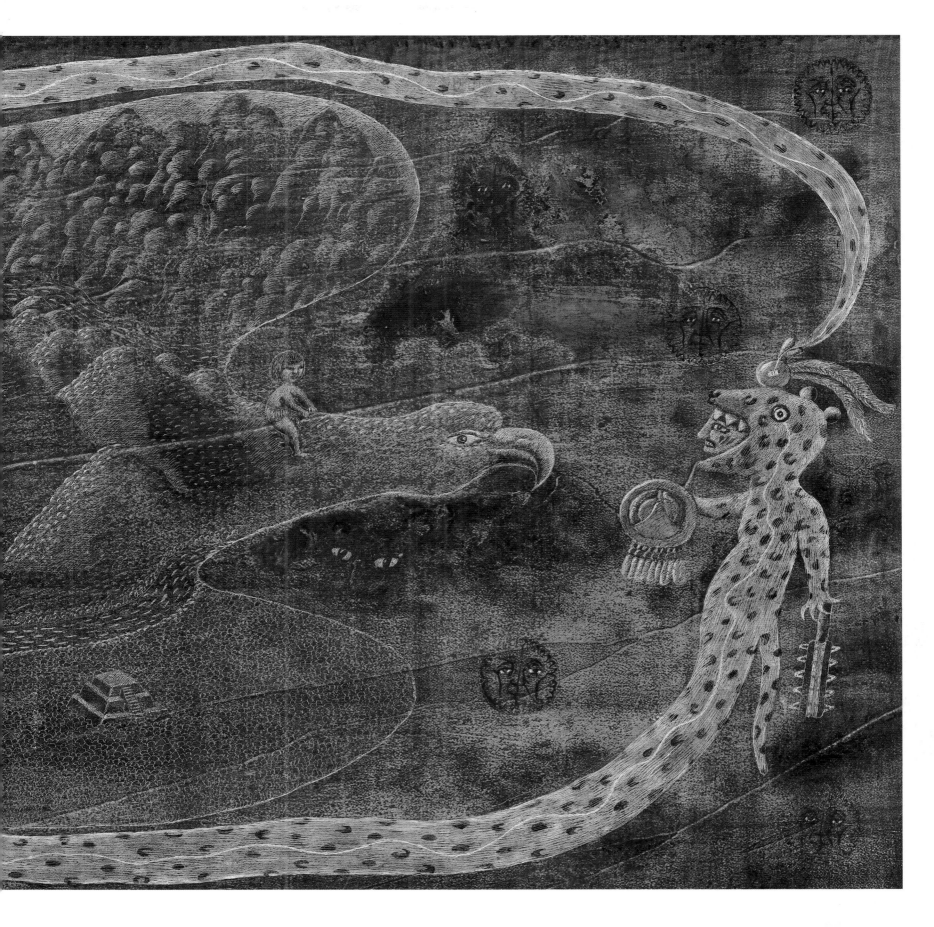

LIONS

T. REX

KOMODO DRAGON

SOMETIMES THEY DANCE

CLEOPATRA IS NAMED AFTER AN EGYPTIAN QUEEN

Hi

CLEOPATRA

MY TOOTH IS LOOSE!

CLEOPATRA IS A SCHOOL FRIEND

RHINO

OCEAN

JUNGLE

THERE ARE SECRET ANIMALS IN THE GARDEN

EAGLES

THEY PRETEND IT IS DESERT

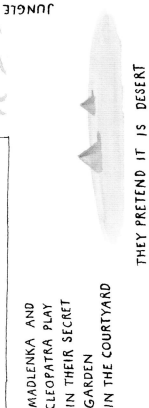

MADLENKA AND CLEOPATRA PLAY IN THEIR SECRET GARDEN IN THE COURTYARD

CLEOPATRA AND ALL THE GIRLS CAN'T WAIT TO LOSE THEIR BABY TEETH AND GROW UP...

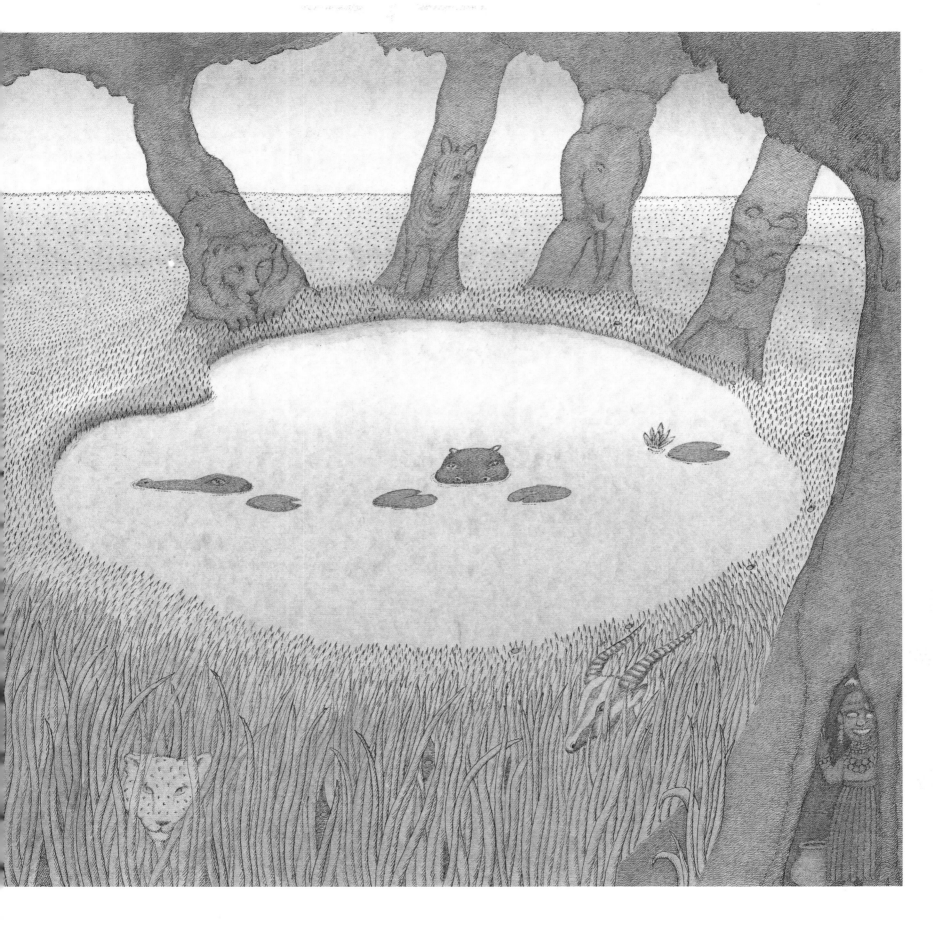

Who else can she tell?

Oh! Mrs. Kham has to know.

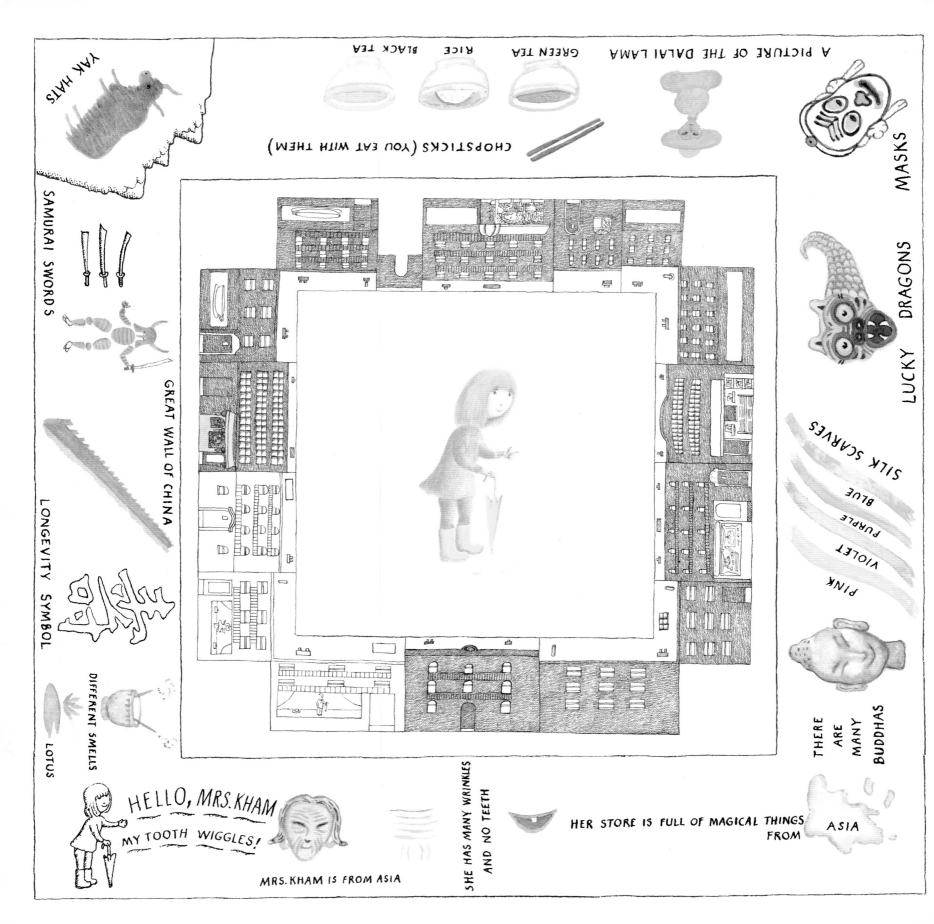

YAK HATS

BLACK TEA

RICE

GREEN TEA

A PICTURE OF THE DALAI LAMA

MASKS

CHOPSTICKS (YOU EAT WITH THEM)

SAMURAI SWORDS

LUCKY DRAGONS

GREAT WALL OF CHINA

SILK SCARVES

BLUE

PURPLE

VIOLET

PINK

LONGEVITY SYMBOL

DIFFERENT SMELLS

LOTUS

HELLO, MRS. KHAM

MY TOOTH WIGGLES!

SHE HAS MANY WRINKLES AND NO TEETH

HER STORE IS FULL OF MAGICAL THINGS FROM ASIA

THERE ARE MANY BUDDHAS

MRS. KHAM IS FROM ASIA

Tashi delek, Mandala. That's a lucky sign.

Oh dear. I'm late.

Madlenka! Where have you been?

Well . . . I went around the world.

And I lost my tooth!

First published in the USA in 2000 by Farrar, Straus & Giroux

First published in the UK in 2000 by Allen & Unwin
Osborne House, 111 Bartholomew Road, London, NW5 2BJ
Phone: (44 171) 482 3546   Fax: (44 171) 482 2723
E-mail: Allanunwin@compuserve.com

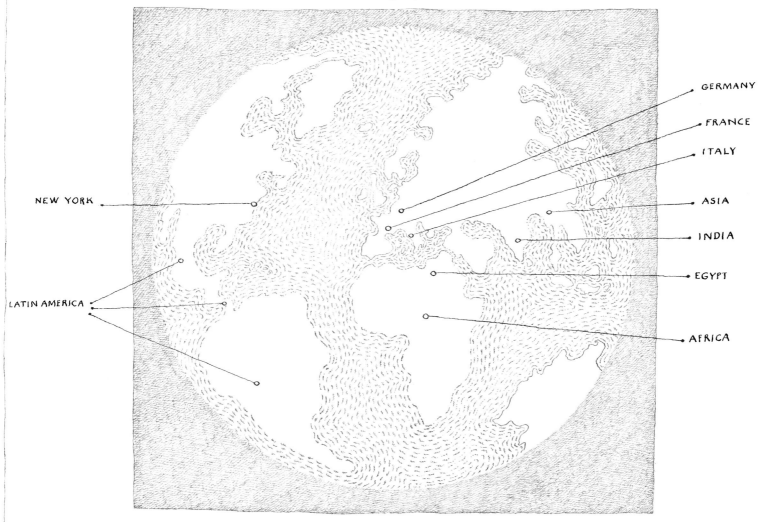

First published in Australia in 2000
by Allen & Unwin
9 Atchison Street
St Leonards, NSW 1590 Australia
Phone: (61 2) 8425 0100
Fax: (61 2) 9906 2218
E-mail: frontdesk@allen-unwin.com.au
Web: http://www.allen-unwin.com.au

National Library of Australia
Cataloguing-in-Publication entry:

Sís, Peter.
Madlenka.
ISBN 1 86508 293 7.
I. Title.
813.54

Published by arrangement with
Farrar, Straus & Giroux

Typography by Filomena Tuosto
Colour separations by Bright Arts (H.K.) Ltd
Printed in Hong Kong by
South China Printing Company (1988) Ltd

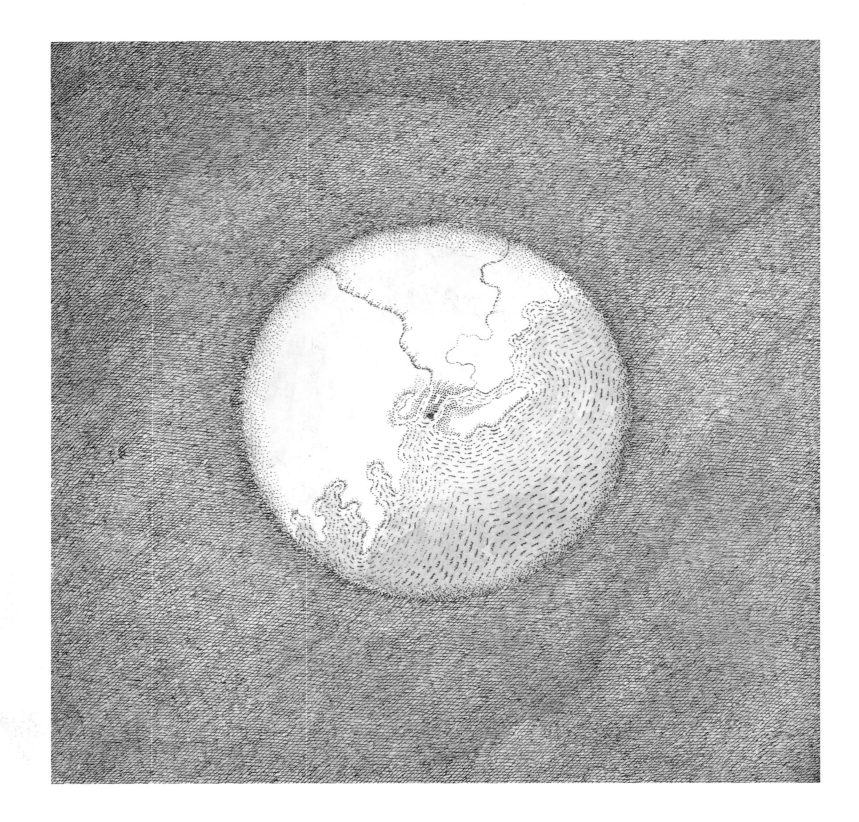